FIVE GLASGOW STORIES

CW01090728

FIVE GLASGOW STORIES

Donal McLaughlin
Christine Appleyard
Carol McKay
Charlie Gracie
Colette Coen

Postbox
PRESS

First published in 2023 by Postbox Press,
the literary fiction imprint of Red Squirrel Press
36 Elphinstone Crescent
Biggar
South Lanarkshire
ML12 6GU
www.redsquirrelpress.com

Edited by Colin Will

Design and typesetting by Gerry Cambridge
gerry.cambridge@btinternet.com

Cover image: Duke of Wellington Statue with
Traffic Cones, Royal Exchange Square, Glasgow
© chrisdorney/shutterstock.com

A CIP catalogue record for this book is available from
the British Library.

ISBN: 978 1 913632 42 7

Red Squirrel Press and Postbox Press are committed
to a sustainable future. This publication is printed in
the UK by Imprint Digital using Forest Stewardship
Council certified paper.
www.digital.imprint.co.uk

Contents

Introduction

Cities, love them or hate them, are where a large proportion of Scotland's population lives, with Glasgow being the largest one. It's not surprising then that the city supports a rich and varied cultural life, and that there are a number of very fine writers living in and around Glasgow.

I was therefore delighted by the response to the *Five Glasgow Stories* project initiated by Sheila Wakefield, Founding Editor of Red Squirrel Press, and of its literary fiction imprint, Postbox Press.

The first thing to say about the stories is that Glasgow, the city itself, is a character in the stories themselves. More than just one character, for there are many facets to the city, many different ways of life reflected in those who live in it, and in the conurbation which surrounds it.

I've tried to show that in my selection for this publication. There are five stories, but there are many Glasgows in them, each distinctive and recognisable.

Thank you to all those who submitted to this publication, and in particular to the excellent writers whose work features in these pages. I hope that readers will enjoy them as much as I do.

Colin Will | Editor | Postbox Press

THIS IS OUR CITY

or

PEOPLE MAKE GLASGOW

9 McLocks stories

Donal McLaughlin

unable to write
5 July 2019

Ye couldn't make this up.

McLocks was walking along what wasn't yet Woodside Place, day after writing a 52-word story, when two guys, turning a corner, were suddenly upon him.

Uni types. *Academics.* One, half the age of the other maybe.

'They say they can't write,' the younger one, passing, said, 'but I say: *fifty* words. Write fifty words, just, by next week when we meet to have a chat.'

A pause followed.

Either that, or the distance between them & McLocks became *out-of-earshot.*

canal dogs
15 July 2019

McLocks & McMens were on the ninth mile of their walk that day when they reached the part of the canal where McMens is just about home & McLocks needs half-an-hour at his ease to get back to Central.

They'd hardly parted when McLocks spotted the kids in kayaks again that McMens & him had seen earlier—being trained in single file by a stickler on a bike. Maybe he was imagining it, but McLocks could feel himself breathe more easily as the kayaks, this time, fanned out ahead & raced into the bend, the paddles going twenty to the dozen.

He walked on & as the water narrowed & straightened again, a big grey dog, the height and build of a greyhound, but not a greyhound, came pounding up behind him & skidded to a halt.

'Awright?' McLocks said, as he often says to dogs that, if the mood took them, could bite a lump out of him.

This time too, the danger passed. The dog looked up, its eyes declared peace & off it took again.

Next thing McLocks knew, a dog that looked like a white wolf but wasn't a white wolf raced past, two jogging owners in its wake, each in a black sports bra & leggings. The wolf that wasn't a wolf ignored their calls, instead built up pace in pursuit of the grey hound, ignoring en route a sausage dog, out with its owner. The man happened to stop & look back, in time— like McLocks—to clock the white wolf reaching

& instantly mounting the grey hound. Graphic wasn't the word for it. McLocks swears the other man blushed & mopped his brow. Vertically challenged, the white wolf might've been; its dick but was in; its front paws, clutching for all they were worth.

McLocks preferred to focus on the dachshund.

Unlike its owner, it was seriously overweight, its too many bellies too near the floor.

'Awright?' McLocks greeted the owner as he approached. Then nodded in the direction of the still-entrenched white wolf.

'Bet you're glad that thing didni do that to *your* dog,' he said. '*Skewered* widni have been the word for it!'

'Can say that again, mate. Sno as if Roxy's got a head for heights either.'

a prick
25 July 2019

On the hottest day of the year so far, predicted to be the hottest ever, McLocks left Hillhead Library at seven-thirty, walked the couple of blocks to Great George Street & crossed to reach what little shade there was before he started to climb it. The heat in the sun was still such, he was regretting wearing jeans that gripped his legs; regretting the strap of his bag tight across his chest; regretting the briefcase (sort-of) high under his arm; regretting his new shades, defo not the best for peripheral vision.

He leaned into the hill that, in the heat, seemed steeper than usual & had passed the halfway point before he glanced up to see others coming down, students led by a guy in a shirt & shorts, a *beanpole* of a guy in a *dress* shirt & shorts, his hands held high above his head, the shirt rolled up to his chin, nearly. Head down again, McLocks continued his ascent; the young guy, his descent, two other friends on his heels— pavement wasn't made for three abreast.

Pavement *really* wasn't made for three abreast & so it soon came to pass that the guy's buff middle blocked McLocks, on whom it dawned too late that the still raised hands were supposed to be a double high-five. Nose-to-nose with a stomach, McLocks—appalled—froze. Left the guy hanging.

'Ye serious, man?' he blurted out before his brain could think even.

'Prick!' the young guy said as McLocks stepped to the left & round him. 'You're a fuckin prick!'

'Naw, you're a prick,' the older boy behind him said, pushing his pal on past.

special
26 July 2019

On the second full day of the new prime minister's premiership, McLocks—who'd got by on two too many caprese salads that week—ended up in Little Italy. The only seat available on his favourite (upper) floor was a stool at a bar-style counter, so he relented & accepted one of the downstairs tables, served by a long padded seat. The gaps between these tables being toty, he'd to choose between disturbing the two West End ladies at the end one, or the young Muslim woman two along. Taking care not to impose, he sat down.

The young woman was wearing what the new prime minister—a matter of months, only, before—had likened to a 'letterbox'; was savouring her food; was the perfect neighbour for someone who wanted to read as he waited, whereas the West End ladies were speaking noisily, excitedly, about their respective chalets on holiday. Somehow, nonetheless, McLocks became engrossed in *Dublin Palms*: the bit about the narrator borrowing history books from the library that, as the card at the back revealed, his late father had also borrowed many years before.

The waitress arrived & McLocks, who'd dithered between the *Carbonara* on the normal menu, but with added spinach & peas, & the

Pasta Special, spaghetti with broccoli & chicken in a creamy garlic & parmesan sauce, decided on the potentially messy latter.

He continued reading. By the time his food arrived, the West End ladies were onto the brother of one, who'd come to stay for a week & not only replaced the wine they'd drunk, but left 'a bunch of notes' on the 'counter' & 'an envelope' for each of his nephews, not that *she*—his sister—would've asked him for 'a bean', whereas... her friend completed the sentence...'others would take the mick & give you nothing.' The young woman, meanwhile, was *between mobiles* (if that's even a thing): discreetly making a call on one, studying the screen of another. When she turned to call for the bill, McLocks caught a glimpse of the gorgeous dark pools she had for eyes. Reader, he melted. He'd no bloody right, he knows, but—and no disrespect!—he melted.

The waitress brought the young woman's bill, said 'Special Pasta,' as she placed it on the table, which meant the young woman had also had the spaghetti with broccoli & chicken in a creamy garlic & parmesan sauce, but had eaten it—McLocks recalled the finesse—much more elegantly than he was currently managing. She put down her card & the waitress disappeared to get the machine. McLocks watched, fascinated, as the young woman, meanwhile, adjusted her veil.

'*Letterbox*, ma effin arse,' he thought.

The young woman paid & got up to leave, brushing—as she slipped through the gap—against the standard bits & pieces on his table. She turned to apologise, with a smile; what became a wee giggle.

'Up fuckin yours, Boris,' McLocks thought, pleased—forty-nine years, nearly, after his own family emigrated—to live in a country

Scotland

that has little truck with Brexit & the E-R-bastarn-G.

zimmer
25 August 2019

Two days before, McLocks had read a review of a Booker long-listed novel that, without that review, wouldn't have interested him. He'd hoped to sneak a peek in Waterstones, but the Argyle Street branch didn't have it in. Shortly before its closing time, he was now trying to catch Sauchiehall.

Stuck at the Four Corners, his progress blocked by the constant flow of traffic, the cars too fast or not far enough apart, he was beginning to think he'd picked the wrong shitin moment to set out. Even the green man was keeping him waiting, so he went round into Union Street, proper, to try to wing it.

At one point, he did almost step out, but then reconsidered—*that bloody bus was too bloody fast*. Same went for the car behind it. He glanced down to his left to check the lights, still a solid green, no sign of amber, spotting too late that, opposite, four or five others had started crossing, the last of them—he saw, once the front two had passed—a forty-(maybe)-something with a zimmer.

billy's brolly
2 September 2019

McLocks & McMens were in the basement cafe of Waterstones Sauchiehall, had been for a while, when McMens said, 'That's Billy Connolly down there, I think.'

McLocks looked down from the gallery, along the full length of the cafe, to see McMens had a point: a Big Yin had joined the queue at the counter; was joking with the women ahead of him. The two members of staff—an Italian, McLocks knew, & a Pole—joined in.

'I wasn't sure it was him till I noticed his sandals,' McMens went on. 'No one else in Glasgow would wear those.'

To the McLocks eyes, the shoes had coloured *stripes*. McMens, from what he said, was seeing *straps*.

Billy was soon giving autographs; signing the back of receipts, for the staff too. He finished & stepped away, leaving his umbrella where he'd hung it on the counter. From their vantage point on the gallery, McMens & McLocks noticed immediately. No one else did.

As they continued to watch, Billy deposited his drink on the closest small table, then fetched a paper from the rack on the one long one. Still, the forgotten brolly went unnoticed.

McLocks—who saw the Big Yin at the Pavilion once: three glorious hours, based on a scrap of paper—was fighting other memories off, he realised. Was trying not to think of recent headlines.

'That first time he turned up on *Parkinson*,' he told McMens instead, 'I'd to *translate* for my mum. Three or four years we were over from Ireland. And I was helpless, laughing, on the floor.'

Time came for McMens & McLocks to leave. Easiest thing would've been to walk round the mezzanine & climb to the ground floor, but neither wanted Billy to lose his brolly.

'You going down to tell him?' McLocks asked. 'Was you spotted him...'

'*I'm* too shy,' he tried to claim when McMens hesitated.

'No, *you* do it,' McMens urged.

They did the detour to the basement—McLocks leading the way down the stairs.

He made straight for the counter & brolly, then approached the man himself.

Question was what to say.

'Mr Connolly, sir—it's yourself, isn't it?' is what came out.

'Yes,' the man confirmed, shaking the hand McLocks had extended.

'You left this at the counter.'

'Oh thanks. I can't go losing that. It's a *hotel* umbrella. —*Thank* you.'

'No, thank *you*,' McLocks tried to say. 'For everything—down through the years,' he added, seeing Billy looking puzzled.

He'd have loved to have a chat but didn't want to impose.

Forty-five years, he thought as McMens & him headed for the stairs beside the lift. Forty-five years, Billy'd been making him laugh.

When he you-tubed it later, it was only forty-four.

sorry we missed you
3 November 2019

McLocks was on his way to see the latest Ken Loach, a *later* screening than first intended. It being a Sunday evening, favourite cafes & bookshops were closing early, so to kill the chunk of time before the next showing, he put in a walk, a just-for-the-exercise walk, to the West End.

En route, the coffee he'd had at Waterstones suddenly hit. No lunch, he remembered. And an even later tea now beckoned. Two eateries came to mind. He opted for the one less likely to be full; where there'd be less fuss; where he could go in, order, eat, make the swiftest of exits & still walk all the way back for the film.

The Hielan Coo burger & halloumi sticks filled a hole (as they say) but the glass of water, lacking the ice he'd specifically requested, remained untouched until he realised that, in the absence of wipes, he could dip his fingers in it. He paid, got ready to go, stepped out onto the street to head back. At the Bank Street junction he used the two green men to cross. At the next corner down, fifty-odd years after learning to, he *looked right, looked left, looked right again...* then, remembering the street in question was one-way, looked left a second time & focused on that direction. The majority of cars on the Great Western Road were whizzing towards the Botanics; the one car waiting to turn was very much stationary; so—*and if all's clear*—McLocks set out for the pavement opposite.

Potholes, admittedly, an *archipelago* of them, caused his final two steps to be faltering, but his peripheral vision, like the eyes in the back of his head, told him that the car that passed behind him passed safely. Only a much-delayed GET AFF THE FUCKIN ROAD YA FUCKIN BASS, screeched by a vision that was half-dog, half-albino, & hanging out the passenger-seat window, caused him to glance back. The young woman, early twenties at most, got no reaction; not even inwardly. No, *undeterred*, McLocks did that thing he always does: put one foot in front of the other, one foot in front of the other just, & kept going.

on growing acceptance
27 November 2019

McLocks had been checking his email in the basement cafe of Waterstones, but not in the "body of the kirk" (as he calls it); naw: over at the big table next to RELIGION. He was flicking through the programme for Celtic Connections, the hard copy he'd forgotten he had in his rucksack, when a striking female voice caught his ear.

He looked up but couldn't see the speaker. Pillar right at his shoulder was blocking his view. Escalator beyond it was a further obstacle. The woman, he guessed, had to be in under the slant, at the round table.

'The *Irish* accent's nice,' she was suddenly saying.

'The *southern* Irish accent,' she specified, dismissing (by implication) McLocks's native north. 'That Irish guy was funny, wasn't he, trying to do the Australian accent...'

The penny dropped. Her monologue wasn't on regional accents. Naw: it was *I'm A Celebrity* the night before, she was on about.

Just months away now from the 50th anniversary of his family's arrival in Scotland, McLocks decided he'd 'take that' (as they say these days); to embrace this increased tolerance of anything Irish.

McLocks, don't forget, was Irish in the 1970s.

inn deep
6 December 2019

McLocks had walked from Central Station to Kelvinbridge in what was left of that day's daylight. Up Hope Street, along Sauchiehall to Charing Cross, over the bridge, along Woodside Place towards Kelvingrove, then down through the park & along the River Kelvin, before a spontaneous detour to the Pocket — where he'd get a far better coffee than where he was originally heading.

'Are you sitting in?' the owner asked. 'Take a seat and I'll bring it over.'

Maybe because it was so dull outside, the Alasdair Grays on the walls forced McLocks — as he neared a table — to look anew; this time, more aware of certain colours. He took a seat beneath the hippo anyway & out came the laptop to do some editing.

A woman was working to his left, her smart-phone concealing the cover of her book. WHO NEEDS WORDS, he spotted on the spine. Author was Richard Little-something. He'd google it later maybe.

His espresso arrived.

The chilled water that came with it was also perfect.

McLocks could have sat there longer, but wanted to continue his walk.

'I'm so used to paying up front,' he confessed, fishing for change at the counter, 'there's always the danger of me leaving without paying.'

'Don't worry, that's what I'm here for!' the owner joked, brandishing his imaginary crook.

Outside, McLocks negotiated the subway station to get to the side of the river he needed. Ahead, a woman—*lazy, or what?*—was walking her dog by bike. McLocks crossed the bridge & where the path narrows outside the bar, suddenly had to do an emergency stop. The dog-walking cyclist had come to a sudden halt—to let oncoming walkers filter past. McLocks watched as the door of Inn Deep swung open, the dog sailed in as someone left, the door swung shut again behind it & the cyclist had to reach across for the handle.

'Looked like it wants a stiff drink!' the walker thus obstructed joked before the dog reappeared.

Trapped behind the cyclist, McLocks started

to fidget as (still) no one moved. Dog then did a runner as the string of male walkers filtered through.

'Raven!' the cyclist called after it.

Raven? McLocks thought. No bloody wonder the thing has taken to drink!

He was through the tunnel & nearing the next bend before the cyclist started cycling again & overtook him. She'd hardly passed when round the bend came a guy in a smart jacket, more interested—McLocks could see—in his quick, guilty swig o summit. McLocks looked on as the two almost clashed. Cyclist had to jerk to her right. Guy hissed some objection to *dog-fuckin-walkers on wheels*. Flustered, clearly; *fumbling*; he returned the half-bottle to his pocket, then staggered on—leaving McLocks alone on the Walkway, to stop, *take it in*, & ponder the muddy bloody chill.

THREE STAGES
OF TWILIGHT

Christine Appleyard

Susan placed her coffee mug beside the pile of travel brochures on the balcony table and looked out over the roaring M90, past the aluminium plated Armadillo, to the hills on the south side of Glasgow. The Alexander 'Greek' Thompson church spires and the merchants' towers overlooking the Clyde were so sharply defined in the clear air, she felt she could reach out and touch them.

During the sixties and seventies, the smog had turned day into night; the Ravenscraig steel-works spewed out sparking flames, turning the sky a diabolical red. Even in daylight it could be difficult to see what was in front of your nose.

There were no descriptions of gaseous steel-works or of the crescendoing animalistic roars from football stadiums in the Enid Blyton books she'd read when she was wee. Cream teas and ginger pop hadn't featured in her family's Sunday outings to the murky pond in Queen's Park where even the swans seemed depressed; she got a dribbling ice cream oyster from the creepy man in the tinkly van and a bottle of Irn-Bru, if she was lucky.

Shielding her eyes, she made out the faint buttery-yellow haze of gorse on the Cathkin Braes.

She remembered a sepia photograph in her Gran's album: ladies in linen dresses, parasols protecting their fine Scottish skin, their backs corset straight, sitting on tartan travelling rugs, applauding moustachioed men in white flannels.

Anyone for Tennis? The Braes 1923

Now the Castlemilk housing estate, or 'Chateau du lait,' as the Glasgow taxi drivers called the vast scheme surrounded the beauty-spot. The tennis courts had been torn up to make way for bouncy trampolines the size of small, unstable planets. Maybe the planners had meant for it to be better than it had turned out. Hindsight was a fine thing.

The library in the council estate precinct had been the only one left open in her neighbourhood at the height of the three-day week. Stray dogs roamed the streets feeding on discarded fish suppers spilling from mountains of fly-blown rubbish left uncollected on the pavement.

Once, she'd walked home, art books under her arm, when a gawky lad with a greyhound that was missing a front leg stopped her on the path across the field to her house. He'd asked her the time. And then he'd exposed himself. Most likely he'd been sniffing glue at the back of the

Cathkin Hotel. When she thought about it, it wasn't his penis clutched in his sticky fist she remembered, it was the greyhound.

Moving from her balcony into the small sitting room she collapsed the clotheshorse and gazed at the picture hanging above the flame-effect gas fire.

She'd just left Art School and, throwing caution and six months' rent to the wind, had bid for the painting in an auction off Garnethill Road. It'd survived her flat shares and the subsequent house moves as she ascended the Snakes and Ladders of the property market.

Ali had said it was too big for her new flat, it needed a larger space, an airy room, to show it off to its best advantage. She looked again at the painting squashed above the mock pine mantelpiece and the artexed ceiling. He was right. You needed to step back to get the right perspective.

Who were these people: the man with the horse and cart, the wee lad at the close door, and the woman staring out of the window, her washing hanging on the drooping grey line. How could she have got her sheets so white? Artistic license perhaps. Susan smiled. She knew all about that.

If she decided to let the painting go, it'd be the woman she'd miss the most. There was a dignity about her, a strength. It felt as if the artist had known these folk intimately. George Walker had been over-looked in his own lifetime, but now his paintings were collected by those who wouldn't know a Gorbals' single-end from the back end of an Edinburgh tram.

She glanced at her watch. Better get herself ready.

The floor to ceiling bedroom mirrors caught her unaware. Multiple versions of herself crowded towards her from every angle, hemming her in. She took a deep breath and stared at her reflection. Who in the name of God wanted to see themselves in such uncompromising detail? It was bad enough with your clothes on, but naked, in the full light of day. She drew the blinds; darkness hid a multitude of sin.

Her mobile phone pinged as she walked back into the sitting room.

BE OUTSIDE IN 5. WON'T COME UP KIDS MIGHT STEAL STUFF

Indeed they might.

The lift smelt of urine and sweet cigarette smoke but at least it was working. She pressed the button. GROUND FLOOR LOBBY. What did they think they'd built, the bloody Ritz?

In the concrete play area surrounding the flats, children wheeled about on thick-tyred bikes like scavenging gulls. She'd bought the twins bikes when they were wee. Not top of the range or anything. No Thank You letter, of course. Her mother had been insistent on good manners, keeping up appearances, even though they lived in a prefab and her dad had enjoyed a light refreshment or two, as they used to say. What would they say now; he'd ongoing issues with the imbibement of alcohol-related substances, or something. Really, he was just an alky: a disappointed man, big on swagger, small in stature, the same as so many Glaswegian men.

Children played different games now, on the computer. In her day they'd stoated hard rubber balls against garage doors

> *First leggy second leggy*
> *jibby and through,*
> *back bridgey burly*
> *and I love you,*

and played skipping games in the street.

> *Murder murder three stairs up*
> *the mannie in the middle door*
> *hut me wae a cup*
> *ma heeds aw broken ma face aw cut*
> *murder murder polis three stairs up.*

Her son's white Range Rover drew up in front of her. Susan waved through the tinted glass and tugged at the door handle.

The window lowered. 'It's electric, Mother, don't yank it like that.'

She'd travelled the route a thousand times, sitting on the top of the number 18 bus clutching a sodden satchel, her damp blazer smelling of her family's old Labrador, gazing at the blackened buildings, the vestiges of an Empire she'd learned about from the oil-cloth maps in cold classrooms: the familiar landmarks of her once flourishing city.

The Land Rover, a sealed unit of silence, navigated the old Glasgow Cross with its clock faces and the city's coat of arms. What was the wee poem?

> *The bell that never rang*
> *the fish that didn't swim*, was that right?
> *The bird that never flew.*

And something about a tree.

She glanced at Ali. 'What does the tree represent, Ali? In the Glasgow poem?'

'Poem? What are you talking about? What poem?'

The Arts were never his thing. Not even nursery rhymes. When he was wee, he'd thrown the *Golden Book of Children's Verse* out of the window, screaming he wanted an Action Man annual.

'It doesn't matter, Ali. I was just thinking about the poem on the coat of arms, that's all. But it doesn't matter.'

Wiping a blur of condensation off the passenger seat window with her buttoned sleeve, she peered out. There was air-con in the car, but she didn't like to ask.

The Rhul Bingo Hall across the street had been a cinema in her day. Technicolour Western posters displayed a grizzled John Wayne and his handsome sidekick, herding long-horn cattle across the Rio Grande, heading to dusty towns and bawdy bars. When it had been covered by a Goldfinger poster, she'd felt as if a part of her soul had been pasted over.

'Here we are.' His voice, so like his father's, pulled her from the fantasy of the Texas sun, back to the grey stone of south-side suburbia.

Alistair jumped from the leather driving seat, strode up the steps and opened the stained-glass front door; etched fruit spilled from a cornucopia of plenty.

Susan followed.

Monday, Tuesday, Wednesday, Thursday, Friday, Saturday, Sunday.

Childhood games. Childish shrieks. The terror of capture and surrender.

Susan slipped off her coat and folded it over her arm. Placing her palm on the cool wall, she gazed up the stairwell toward the roof light. 'Oh, you've had the hallway painted.'

'Yes. Farrow and Ball, 'Polar Bear's Pelt'. It cost a fortune. We like the chalkiness of the white.'

She remembered her husband's drawn face as he stood in the same hallway, yelling directions at the men from Pickford's.

'Polar Bear's Belt, Ali, well...that is...different.'

> *Yesterday upon the stairs I met a man*
> *   who wasn't there,*
> *he wasn't there again today,*
> *I wish that man would go away.*

How could she make light of it. Hugh's temper was never a joke. She remembered the feel of the worn leather belt as she tried to yank it out of his clenched hand when he removed it from the thin loops on his ill-fitting trousers. He believed in discipline. Thought that his son should be disciplined, in the same way as he had been, in his boarding school, up in that unforgiving Scottish Glen.

'What? What?'

'The Polar Bear, Ali. The Polar Bear's belt.'

'For God's sake mother, *pelt*. Polar Bear's *pelt*.'

'Oh, yes. I see. Well, that is clever isn't it. Do you think they skinned the Polar Bear and sold the pelt?'

'What? Who? For Heaven's sake what are you

talking about now? It's just the name of the bloody paint!'

'Ah, yes, the name of the bloody paint.'

The new kitchen looked out into the garden, sliding glass doors led onto wooden decking.

'It all looks lovely, Ali.' Susan turned, hanging her coat over the high spindle-backed chair. 'You and Penny must be delighted with everything you've acquired.'

'Yes, we are. Hard work of course. But I'm not afraid of hard work, and neither is Penny. Although she is working part-time now. Dad instilled the need for hard work in me from an early age, hard work and discipline. As you know.'

'Yes.' Susan gazed out, through the fragile glass boundary, onto the unfamiliar garden. 'Your father always did have a strong sense of both.'

They'd met at a city secondary school when he'd interviewed her for a temporary teaching post.

> *Oor wee school's the best wee school, the*
> *best wee school in glesga*
> *the only thing that's wrang wi it is the*
> *baldy heeded maister*
> *he goes tae the pub oan a saturday nicht*
> *'n goes tae church on sunday*
> *tae pray tae god tae gie hum strength*
> *tae belt awe the weans oan monday.*

Art wasn't a priority at the school, as he'd explained, but he needed a qualified teacher to tick the right boxes. God, she'd been naïve. Straight from Art School, straight from a failed relationship with the lascivious art lecturer— Brutalist Art in the Urban Environment—to an inner-city school, and the bed of a thrusting young headmaster.

Matrimony, child, miscarriage. A failed relationship, uncoupled by an unexpected embolism.

One potato two potato three potato four,
five potato six potato seven potato more,
you are out with a dirty rottin clout
right ower your face...
just like this!

'And where's Penny? And the twins? I haven't seen them for ages. I thought they'd be here. Aren't they coming?'

'Of course.' He moved towards the reclaimed Belfast sink, filled the kettle. 'Just off to pick up some things from Waitrose. We're having friends round for dinner tonight. I'm making a coffee. Do you want one?'

She stared at the back of his head, felt the familiar tingle of unexpressed rage prick her scalp. 'If it's not too much trouble.'

'D'you want a biscuit?' He rummaged in the

tin, 'Only got digestives left. Happy Birthday by the way.'

A digestive biscuit. A bloody digestive biscuit. After all she'd done. Staying with his father, keeping up appearances, handing over the house to accommodate his growing family, moving to that tiny flat, for a bloody McVitie's digestive biscuit and a mug of instant coffee. She thought, for once, they would have managed a homemade cake and a bottle of red.

> *Does yer ma drink wine*
> *does she drink it all the time*
> *does she get a funny feelin' when her*
>   *belly hits the ceiling...?*

But no, a stale biscuit and coffee as weak as dirty bathwater. Well, at least now she knew exactly where she stood. She'd more than done her bit, if she sold the painting, there'd be absolutely no guilt.

Sipping her coffee, she smoothed the creases from her dress. 'Thank you, Ali. Yes, a digestive would be...fine.'

'So'. His knee bounced, sploshing coffee over the table.

'So, how're things at the flat?'

Susan nibbled the edge of her biscuit. 'Fine, everything's fine at the flat. Settling in. Some of the neighbours are...interesting.'

'Good. Yes, that's good.' He brushed an imaginary crumb from his knee onto the slate floor. 'And your things? Enough room for all your things?'

Enough room for her things? What things? The things she'd taken to the dump when he'd encouraged her to downsize.

'Well thanks for asking, Ali. Very thoughtful. It's absolutely fine, what with the fitted wardrobes and the magnolia.' She sipped her bitter coffee.

'And how about the picture? Are you finding it a tad depressing, what with all that working-class squalor? Penny was just saying that some nice Japanese prints would suit the space better. More minimal.'

She gazed at her son. Nice Japanese prints. More minimal. Christ, he had literally no idea. Just like his bloody father. 'I'm no great fan of Japonica thank you Alistair, whatever its dimensions.'

'Yes, well, I suppose going to Art School does leave some sort of mark on you.' His mobile's ringtone pierced the suburban silence. He grabbed it from his chinos' pocket, strode across the floor, stabbed the green button, and tugged open the folding glass doors. Warm air carried with it the sound of lawnmowers, the scent of cut grass and melting tar.

'What? No. Not yet. Christ, keep your voice

down. OK I was just about to actually. Yes, later. See you later.'

'That sounded like Penny. Is she on her way? Nothing wrong, I hope.' She glanced at her son. 'You're looking awfully red, Ali, is it the heat?'

'Wrong? No, not at all. Nothing's wrong. Do you want to go into the sitting room? It's cooler in there, north facing.'

North facing? What was he on about, surely not the damned Polar Bears again. 'No, I'm fine Ali. Very comfortable. Quite at home in fact.'

'So...I wanted to talk to you about... It's roasting in here. Hot as hell.'

She waited.

'The twins are both starting at Craighall next month. We're delighted, of course, that they've got in...'

'Your Dad used to say that all you needed to get into that school was a father who could write a cheque. He could be quite amusing sometimes, your father.'

'Could he? Yes...well, he could be many things.' He slumped down opposite her. How much did he remember? Not much surely, he was only a child after all. And he'd adored his father, hadn't he.

'Anyway, the thing is, the fees are quite expensive. Not undoable of course. But expensive.' He raked his hands through his thinning hair.

'I see, Ali.' Susan traced a tight circle with

her finger on the warm wooden table. 'Well, I'm very glad the fees are doable. That must be a relief to you.'

He looked like that swan in the pond when children threw hunks of *Mothers Pride* at its bent head. Unruffled on the outside but paddling furiously below the murky surface.

'Yes, it is a relief. It's a relief that we can just about afford to send our children to a school where they can be themselves, feel safe.'

Sunlight caught the mock Rennie Macintosh clock on the wall.

'Good. That's good, feeling safe is important. Anyway, I need to go to the bathroom before I leave you. If you'll excuse me?'

The old Armitage Shanks had been ripped out, the original cast iron bath replaced by a walk-in shower and matching vanity units.

Susan sat on the oak toilet seat. The suddenness of Hugh's stroke. Watching him as he struggled to get out of the bath. He would've hated to die like that. Undignified. Vulnerable. His penis, like a sea slug, wafting in the cold scummy water.

> *I had a little monkey his name was Tiny Tim*
> *I put him in the bath to see if he could swim*
> *he drank all the water*

he ate all the soap
and he died last night with a bubble in
  his throat.
With a bubble in his throat.
He died last night, with a bubble in his
  throat.

Down the stairs, into the kitchen, a quick 'chee-rio'.

Exit stage left. Followed by bears. Out of the etched door and into the garden.

Sunday Saturday Friday Thursday
Wednesday Tuesday Monday.

The bus crossed the Clyde on the George V bridge. The Waverley steamer chugged tourists out towards the mouth of the river, past the M90, and the Merchant City. The Armadillo, claws retracted, crouched on its silted bank. Susan took in the view of the city from the top deck. It wasn't the view she'd dreamt of, but perhaps, if she sold the painting, she'd have options. Just a matter of testing the water. She sat back, luxuriating in the familiar heat of the leatherette seat, thinking about her hidden poster, about crossing the Rio Grande, under the blazing Texan sun.

LOOK UP

Carol McKay

'Jist look up!' Ah yelled. Then Ah tossed his dirty pants at him.

The door slammed an his pants slid doon it tae the flair. Ah held ma fists in front ae me an squeezed an squeezed till ma nails left marks in ma palms. There wis double lines under the skin ae ma wrists an Ah wished Ah could scoot out streams ae sticky spider silk an swing ma wey through canyons between fifty storey office blocks an high rises in the daurk jist tae get oot ae here. Bit it wis daylight, an there wisnae any fifty storey office blocks in Possil: jist a labyrinth ae shite-brown tenements an terraced houses.

Who knew when Billy'd be back? His maw wis right. He wis never gonnie man-up enough tae be a faither. She'd know. She'd had three kids tae three different men an no wan ae thum hung roon lang enough tae set a guid example. Ah could hardly blame Billy fur no huvin a da. Ah could hardly blame Billy fur anythin. No haein a job—that wisnae his fault when there wis naethin except care work wi aw the factories shut doon, an who could blame him fur blanchin at the thought ae wipin arses? Ah tellt him there wis mair tae it than that—aw they auld blokes lookin fur companionship—bit he didnae get it.

Ah checked ma phone. There wis still time fur the washin afore ma shift. Tae be honest, pickin up his pants an tryin tae work oot where he'd left his other sock this time wisnae the best way tae keep ma mind aff the nausea, bit stormin through the hoose dulled ma temper. Billy's maw hud him ruined. That wis what Jade said. Jade wis a care assistant like me bit she wis only daein it fur a year tae save up fur Australia. Ah'd said tae Billy, 'We could pit oor wages thegither an work oot a budget, spend the minimum oan food an electric, an pit the rest in the credit union. By the end ae the year we could fly tae Oz like Jade's daein.' Or jist go oan holiday. Bit wis he buyin it?

The last few times Ah'd used it, this washin machine rumbled like wan ae they auld-fashioned drums fur tombola. Ah shoved the socks an pants in then sorted oot the pile fae the wash bag in the bedroom. As ever, he'd left his jeans haulf inside-oot, so Ah had tae push ma erm up wan leg tae pull it back the right way roon. There wis a bettin slip in his poaket. Ah crushed it an threw it at the bin. Ah felt the anger build up again an knew Ah should stoap goin ower it: accept him as he wis or move oan. Bit could Ah? Especially noo it wis even mair complicated?

Ah stuffed the jeans in an reached fur his tee-shirts. Ah'd ask Billy wan mair time tae look at the washin machine. Pity it wisnae a caur engine; he wis guid at workin oot how tae make *them* go. Pity he loast his licence an his apprenticeship wae it, bit life wis shite an ye hud tae get oan wae it. Nane ae this mopin aroon, believin ye wur born unlucky. That's whit Jade tellt me.

Ah'd said tae him, 'If we go tae Australia ye might get a joab drivin.' Drivin wis a transferable skill—like care workin. Everybidy aeways needs drivers an care workers. We could huv it made, him an me. Ah tellt him that—mair than wance—bit he jist wrinkled up the side ae his mooth an said dross like us didnae get anywhere. Dross like us! That made me mad.

Ah needed tae get up aff ma knees. Ha! Ah leaned oan the machine an looked oot the windae. Nae sign ae him. There wis absolutely naebidy oot in the scheme: no even a dug or a blackbird. Naethin. Except that deid fly oan the windae sill. Poor fly. Ah actually felt fur it. It hid been lookin fur a wey oot, an Ah wis, tae. Noo it wis a smear wae a wing broken aff.

It wis right gloomy oot there. Ah could jist make oot the tap ae the church spire at St Theresa's. Think ae the view ye'd huv fae there! That's whit Jade says. Ye could see for miles—up ower the silvery lines ae the canal an the motorwey, an aw the wey intae the centre ae Glesga, an beyond it tae the braes in the distance. There's braes aw roon Glesga, wan ae the auld guys said. There's a lot ae rain, tae, Ah said, laughin, an giein him his tea. Bit he came right back an said that's whit makes it the dear green place. Jade wis noddin in agreement. Ah jist shrugged. Ah hadnae much experience ae it, jist steyin in Possil. Mibbe Ah should get oot mair. Ah wondered whit it wid be like in Australia. Ah'd heard it wis hot an sunny. Ah'm no very keen on hot temperatures. Jade said there wis big deserts, bit the coastal toons wis lush an beautiful.

Billy wouldnae buy intae ma dreams. He said ma heid wis fu ae crazy foam, bit how come it wis him spendin his days watchin telly, an it wis me daein the washin afore ma shift at the care home? Ah pit ma heid oan ma erms oan the worktap. Aw ma insides wis curdlin. Ah didnae mean ma mornin tae turn intae a bickerin rant. The nausea wis bad enough withoot that. Mibbe in Australia he'd get anither chance at becomin a mechanic. He said naw: Australia wantit people who wis *already* mechanics. Whit goat me maist wis that he didnae even try.

Noo, this. Ah thought back tae earlier in the mornin. The day hud goat aff tae a guid stert, wae Billy pokin his fingers in ma middle, makin me jump an giggle. Then the postman brought a letter: fae the hospital, giein the date fur ma scan. Billy reached it afore me. There it wis, wi

'NHS' aw ower it. He opened it while Ah wis bilin the kettle.

'Whit's this?' he said, staunin in the kitchen doorway. He shook the letter. 'When wis ye thinkin ae tellin me?'

Ah drew a deep breath. 'Sorry, Billy. It's jist— Ah'm no sure how Ah feel aboot it.'

'Whit?' Billy's eyes near disappeared in a scowl, an it looked like some guy wae a knife had gouged lines in his foreheid. Then he said, 'In that case, mibbe ye'd better get rid ae it.'

Ma hert raced. Ah clutched at ma fingers; Ah clutched at ma options. 'Ah'm no sure, but. Ah'll get maternity pay,' Ah said. 'Then ma maw can look efter the wean. Or yours.'

He stood there, lookin doon.

'Or we can pit him in a nursery.'

It wis that hard tae read him. 'So, whit wis aw that fantasy aboot Australia?'

Ah felt ma bottom lip wobble. 'Ah'm sorry. Ah jist fell pregnant.'

'Jist "fell"?'

Ah leaned ma weight oan the back ae a chair, aware ae the cloth ae ma tunic pulsin wi the beat ae ma hert. Billy wisnae bein fair. 'Okay, no jist "fell". No immaculate conception. It wis an accident.' Ah felt masel grouw angry. 'Bit you hid quite a bit tae dae wi it.'

He shook oot the letter again. 'Sure aboot that?'

Whit? Ah nearly gret. 'Of course Ah'm sure. Onywey, ye shouldnae hae opened ma letter.'

He stuffed it back in the envelope an thrust it oot tae me. Ah took it in shaky hauns an fixed it.

Billy stood wi his erms foldit, watchin me. 'So, if Ah cannae even pit a letter back in its envelope, whit kin ae faither d'ye think Ah'd be?'

'Och, Billy.' Ah'd sat doon, feelin light-heided. Did Ah huv tae be reassurin him aw the time? 'Ye jist need tae get used tae the idea.'

His mouth crimped. 'Nah. Look, Zoë. Ah huvnae git a joab.' He ran his haun ower his heid. 'You're oan a sixteen hour contract. Yer mother's chippin in oan the bills as it is. How could we afford a wean? You're the wan that needs tae get used tae the idea.'

He'd made it sound like Ah wis askin fur a puppy. Ah wanted tae tell him about climbin up tae the tap ae that spire an lookin roon, bit he'd jist say Ah wis dreamin again, so Ah steyed doon tae earth. 'Ah'll go back tae work early. Ah'll get mair oors,' Ah said, an reached oot tae him. 'You could be workin by then.'

'Aye, right,' he said, an twisted awey. 'Ye know there's nothin.'

'There's care work.'

That fly had zig-zagged between us. We watched it fur a minute then he picked up the dish towel an slapped it oan the windae pane. The fly lay belly up, legs wrigglin.

Aw Ah could think wis how unhygienic it wis. Ah grabbed the towel aff him an threw it oan the flair in front ae the washin machine. 'Ye'd be better daein care work than watchin telly or spendin your benefit in the bookies.'

'An you'd be better goin tae the doctor's. Tell him this thing's scramblin yer brains an ye need tae get rid ae it.'

'Aww, jist look up, Billy!'

That wis when he stomped oot an Ah threw his dirty pants at him.

The thing wis: Billy wisnae a bad person; he wis jist brought up in bad circumstances. It crippled his confidence. If everybidy says ye're worthless—yer maw, yer teacher, yer gran— how ur ye ever gonnie believe ye're no? Bit he did need tae take responsibility. That wis somethin the auld men at the care home could teach him. They'd gie him confidence; be guid role models. An they'd love his humour. If only he would risk it.

There wis that fly, still belly up oan the windae sill. Ah tore aff a sheet ae kitchen towel, wiped up the bits ae fly an binned it. Then Ah goat back oan ma knees tae sort through the rest ae the washin: two pairs ae ma work troosers an a couple ae dark tunics. Ah patted doon the poakets automatically an took oot a latex glove an a tissue. Then Ah minded wan ae the auld men had gied Jade an me each a scratch caird. He'd bought wan fur Jade, really, because he knew she wis goin tae Australia, bit because we worked as a team he said he couldnae leave me oot. Jade gave him a big cuddle—that wis why she wis everybidy's favourite—bit Ah wis mair reserved. Ah wis worried it wid be a breach ae ethics tae take somebidy's scratch caird. Like takin money? Ah fun it in the poaket ae ma tunic an pit it oan the worktap then closed the door an poured in soap powder. Ah chose the short programme so it wid be done afore Ah left fur work, an prayed the machine wid last another few cycles.

Ah glanced at the scratch caird. 'Beginner's luck', it said, an ye had tae find a drawin ae a horseshoe tae win the prize. It hud only cost a pound, so it wisnae highway robbery. Onywey, whit wis the chances? Oan the back, it said the biggest prize wis £7,000, bit the odds must be a million tae wan. Ah thought aboot it while Ah wis makin ma pieces, an toast an ham tae eat afore work, avoidin fat tae ease the nausea. Ah thought aboot it while Ah stirred ma tea.

Ah could git a new washin machine fur a stert. It gurgled while Ah sat at the table an ate lunch. Ah could buy a pram, an a cot an bath fur ma baby. Clothes an nappies an a high-chair. That lot wid cost a fortune. Ah glanced oot the windae again an thought aboot the other option. Ah minded masel there *wis* another option. Ah could gie Billy up, an his baby, an make a brand new stert in Australia.

'Are ye no scared?' Last week oan our tea-break Ah asked Jade the question, an she said, 'Listen, Zoë: life disnae come wi guarantees. Sometimes ye huv tae risk it.' Jade's maw dumped her when she wis wee. She spent her life in an oot ae care homes.

Jist then, Ah heard Billy's key in the door. The dry toast stuck tae the roof ae ma mooth an Ah struggled tae swalley.

The truth wis—Ah wantit Billy. Ah want Billy an his baby. Ah pit ma haun oan ma belly. Mibbe Ah wis the wan that needed tae risk it. This baby wisnae planned, bit sometimes that wis the way life wis. Billy hadnae been planned, bit that didnae mean he wisnae wantit, or that he wis worthless. Except, he probably thought he wis, since that wis whit everybidy tellt him.

He hardly met ma eyes when he came intae the kitchen.

'There's tea in the pot,' Ah said, tryin tae keep ma voice normal.

He filled a cup, let it overflow then reached fur the dishtowel tae wipe it. It wisnae oan the hook, a course, because Ah'd tossed it by the machine efter he'd used it tae kill that fly.

'There's a clean cloth under the sink,' Ah said, an watched him reach in fur it.

He rummaged, displacin half a dozen things wi no thought tae tidy them. He wiped the spill an tossed the cloth in the sink. Then he spotted the scratch caird. 'Where did ye get that?' he said. He pulled oot his chair an sat across fae me at the table.

Ah tellt him aboot the auld man wantin tae help Jade oot wi Australia.

'An he gied you wan, tae? How?'

Ah shrugged. 'Cause he's a decent guy? They're people. They're no jist bums that need wiped.'

'Aye, aye. Ah get it.' The machine gurgled. He tapped his nails oan his mug. 'Are ye no gonnie scratch it?'

'In a minute. Ah wis enjoyin thinkin aboot aw the things Ah could dae if Ah won it. The dreamin's the best part, int it? The anticipation.'

'You're definitely a dreamer.' He held ma eyes wi his deep brown wans. Then he blinked. 'But funnin oot ye're a winner's better.' He leaned back, squeezed his fingers intae his jeans' poaket an brought oot a coin. Typical Billy.

There wis six 'games' oan it. Under each wan wis a picture. Ah scratched aff the silver coverin the first wan an revealed a lucky rabbit's foot. There wis a rainbow under the second. The third an the fourth had pictures ae a spider.

'A spider? What's lucky aboot that?' Billy said, an sniffed. Ah didnae tell him Ah'd dreamed ae sprayin oot spider silk an swingin ma wey awey atween fifty storey buildings. 'Come on: two left. Whit are ye lookin fur? A horseshoe?'

I reached ma haun across the table tae touch

Billy's, expectin him tae draw back. He nearly did, bit he stoapt hissel. 'Billy,' Ah said, 'I don't need luck or money. Ah've got you, an we're haein a baby. We'll get by. People always huv. Look at yer maw.'

He wis quiet fur a minute then he lifted ma haun, turned it ower an ran his rough thumb ower ma wrist. 'Exactly. Look at ma maw. D'ye no think Ah want somethin better?'

Ah studied him an felt somethin rise in ma stomach, bit fur wance it wisnae sick. Ah got it noo. 'But this is better. It's you, me, an this baby.' That scowl flickered ower his features, bit Ah pictured Jade an kept goin. 'Jade says we've no jist tae dream: we've tae *aspire*. An, see the auld guys at the hame? They say life's like gamblin. Sometimes ye huv tae jist risk it.' Ah tried tae get back tae the humour fae the mornin; added ma other haun tae the tap ae his. 'You're usually quite intae the gamblin.'

He pursed his lips. 'An you want this baby?'

'You an this baby.' The room went bright suddenly. Sunshine in Possil? 'Ah'm no really carin aboot Australia,' Ah tellt him, an it wis true. 'Ah mean, it would be nice, bit we could huv a guid life here.' Ah follaed his eyes back tae the scratch caird.

'This auld guy that gies oot lottery tickets— does he make a habit ae it?'

Ah went tae discuss the ethics, tae talk about

integrity, an aboot the care home rules, bit he squeezed ma haun hard an Ah shut up.

'See, ma jokes are wastit,' he said, his face twistin like a smile. 'Those auld guys you work wi must miss a young guy wi good banter. Is that whit ye're sayin?'

Ah kept ma voice quiet, no wantin tae jinx it, bit Ah met his eyes an said, 'Ah'd pit money oan it.' The machine went intae a spin an Ah raised ma voice above it. 'We can dae this, Billy. We jist need tae work towards it. Dream mair. *Aspire.*'

'Aye,' he said. He droapt ma haun an tapped the table beside the scratch caird. 'Still got two chances, furst, but. Get scratchin.'

IF YE KNOW

Charlie Gracie

First time back since Sandy's funeral. Big Tony was there too, said he'd give me a bell if a ticket came up for a gemm. Ferr play tae him, he phoned me a couple ae days ago for the night.

Ahv come through early tae try an catch Eileen. No seen her for ages. She wisnae at the funeral, they never really knew each other. More a pal ae mine than the rest ae the family.

Billy's on a bench in his front garden when ah pass, same place he ayeways is. He disnae look any different fae when we were at school thegither. Apart fae the baldy napper. Ah spied him durin the funeral an we'd a wee quick hya at the purvey. Second time ahv met him in six weeks after twenty-five years. Used tae be great pals too, me an him.

'Right mate?'

'Aye. Yersel?'

He stands up, wanders up tae the gate.

'Ye lookin for Eileen?'

'Aye. Headin doon tae big Tony's bit, thought ahd look in.'

'She's in the Royal, mate. Fell doon the sterrs.'

'Right?'

'Belter too, fucked her heid at the bottom.'

'Jesus.'

'Aye, lucky me an Susan were there. Right time, right place. She sorted her oot an ah called the ambulance.'

'Man alive.'

'Lucky.' He swigs fae his mug. 'Fortnight nearly.'

'What ward?'

'Dunno, mate. No managed in yet.'

Tony pulls away fae the lights on Alexandra Parade. It came on rain when ah got tae his bit, so once ah worked oot how tae find the ward, the big fella offered tae run me in.

Good guy that way.

Ah owe him.

'Fancy a wee coffee at Celino's, mate?'

'You no think you should go an see Eileen first but?'

'Aye, ah suppose, but a wee stop in Celino's'll be good.'

He's got me the ticket for the gemm an noo he's runnin me in tae see Eileen—least ah can do.

'Plenty time. Ahl still get intae see her before we go tae the gemm.'

'She'll appreciate seein ye,' says Tony.

'Aye,' ah say. 'Fawin doon the sterrs, fuck.'

An affogato in Celino's, ma treat. Tony's never

heard ae it even, but once convinced tae try it, he's as much a fan as me.

'Brilliant, mate.'

When we're done, he drops me at the entrance tae the Royal.

'Ah better get up the road, mate,' he says. 'Need tae get a bite tae eat an pick up the tickets. Then ahl be headin.' He looks at me funny. 'Get back tae me sharp so we meet up, right.'

He shouts me back as soon as ah walk away.

'You definitely on for it, Allan?'

'Course,' ah say. 'Ahl no be that long up here. In an oot.'

It's wan ae the wards in the old Royal, windaes covered wi a film tae keep the sun oot ae folks' eyes. Just like Mammy was in that time they thought she'd a heart attack, but it turned oot it was just a burst ulcer.

Eileen's lyin on top ae the covers, wrapped in a red housecoat. She smiles her big smile an shuffles roon, puts her haun oot tae greet me.

'When'd ah last see you, son?'

'Just before Covid. Two or three year?'

'Never. Must be five anyway.'

'Naw, seriously. Mind ah came up tae the hoose wi oor Louise an she brought wee Matthew wi her an you an him were playin wi the budgie?'

Eileen says, 'Oh aye,' an strains tae look oot ower the glare screen. 'What time is it?'

'About hauf six.'

'At night?'

'Aye. Ahm meeting Tony McGowan for the gemm.'

'Celtic?'

'Who else?'

She laughs.

'The McGowans fae Ash Road?'

'That's him,' ah say.

'Nice big fella that. Ah was at school wi the oldest one. Wullie McGowan. Liked him and aw.'

'Aye. Tony's the second youngest.'

'Seven ae them ah think,' she says.

A young woman walks into the ward an heads straight for us. Ah know ah should know who she is but ah cannae place her.

'Hya Auntie Eileen.'

'Hya pet.'

She lifts her haun, smiles.

'Are you Stephen?'

'No, that's ma brother. Ahm Allan, the older wan.'

'Cool. I'm Amanda.'

'Oh aye, Raymond's lassie. Should've guessed, lookin at ye, shape ae your face.'

'That's what everybody says.'

Eileen shuffles tae the edge ae the bed an sits up straight.

Amanda hands her a packet ae Tuc biscuits.

'Shouldn't be givin you these, but one or two'll no kill you.'

Eileen laughs an puts them under her pillow. 'Ahl just… tuck them in here.'

She laughs again. 'Get it? Tuck?'

Amanda aims a slap at her heid.

'Your patter's mince, you.'

Eileen rubs her hands thegether, then reaches oot tae me for a fist pump.

'Get her every time, so ah dae.'

Her wee punch is feeble.

'Laugh a blinkin minute, you,' says Amanda.

She takes a bottle ae dilutin juice fae her bag an puts it on top ae the locker.

'You been eatin, Auntie Eileen?'

'Aye, no bad.'

'You have tae or you'll no get home.'

'Ahm happy here.'

'Well, we'll see what happens. I've been up an sorted the flat, but you'll have tae let someone in tae keep it clean.'

'Ah can manage that masel.'

'You can't.'

'Ahl be fine.'

'But you've no *been* fine but.'

Amanda has walked doon fae the ward wi me, filled me in on what's been going on wi Eileen, an we swap numbers before she scoots back up the sterrs again. Ah head oot ontae the High Street.

Ahv been longer than ah meant tae. Stories fae wur childhoods an when Eileen babysat us lot, me an her swappin mad tales, Amanada pishin hersel at the antics. Eileen telt us things about ma da ah never heard before. Brilliant.

Well after hauf seven noo. Ah try tae phone Tony as ahm rushin doon the road, but ah cannae raise him. When ah get tae the Cross, there's a ping fae the phone. He's gied the ticket tae his niece that stays on Springfield Road.

Fuck him.

Ah text it.

Fuck you

Two laughin emojis come back, tears runnin.

Sorry mate ye left me hanging, goney miss the start

Fuckin wank.

Ah text that.

Wank

Nae reply this time.

Ah went tae Babbity's, but ah left sharpish. That's where they aw go after the gemm an ah wouldnae be able tae stop masel if Tony pitched up. Ah was just goney get the bus hame, but somehow ahv ended up sittin on the grass at the Clyde wi a bag ae cans, talkin tae some guy that's lit a fire on the edge ae the river. Cannae even mind how ah got here.

It's quiet, just the two ae us, either side ae the flames, hardly talking noo. Up till a few minutes ago we'd been gassin about bands we'd seen, pubs we used tae go tae, but noo we're silent.

No sure yet if it's a bad silence or a good silence but.

Ah only meant tae go tae Babbity's for a few pints an then up the road. That was the plan. But ah ended up at the offy. First time in ages too.

Ah haun a can tae the guy an spark wan for masel.

'Crackin fire, mate.'

'Aye.'

We're no too far fae the road, but it's secluded. There's a path somewhere up the rise there, where ah came doon an seen the glow ae the fire. Brian's fire.

We're talkin again.

Turns oot Brian lived beside ma Uncle Peter's ma. Ayeways the same when yer oot in this end ae the city. A village just.

We know some other people.

Wullie somebody that ran a studio at Charing Cross, him an his wife, Claire or somethin.

Teresa Scott, who used tae live in Dalmarnock, next street tae Brian, an then moved up tae ma bit when she was in Primary 7. Ah cannae mind what happened tae her.

Ah ask Brian if he can.

'Fucked if ah know,' he says. Stares into the fire again. 'Fucksake.'

Trevor Tierney too, but everybody knows him.

'He's a cunt,' says Brian.

Ah don't say anything about it. Ah know he's a cunt too, but that's better left alone. Especially when you're sitting in the early hours at the Clyde having a few scoops at a fire wi a guy you only met a wee while ago.

Never know where it might lead.

Ah wake up in a blur ae sun fae a windae. Ahm on a couch.

Thank fuck.

Could be worse.

There's a loud snore fae somewhere.

Ahm tryin tae think back tae last night. Whose couch it is.

Brian, that's it. Fire Guy.

The place is a coup. Nae surprise there, kind ae like ma flat after a night on the sauce. Art work on the wall but. All ahv got is ma da's Sacred Heart an a photo ae the Squinty Bridge. Sandy took it an got a copy blown up for me. Pride ae place it has too.

Ah sit up. There's a mad paintin above the fire place, a bright orange explosion, an abstract thing that startles me at first, like it's come oot fae inside *me* or somethin.

A flashback tae durin the night. Brian's punchin it, no sayin nuhin, just hittin an hittin it till it faws off the wall.

That's aw ah can mind. One ae us must ae put it back up but.

Ah get up fae the couch, check ma wallet an ma phone are still in ma pocket, an let masel oot intae the close an doon the sterrs. Don't even go for a slash in case ah wake that Brian up.

It's Duke Street ahm in, corner ae Hunter Street. The close stands almost on its own, wi a pointed turret. When ah look up tae the second floor, Brian's staring oot. Right at me. Ah wave up, point tae ma wrist. No sure he even sees me.

Ah check ma phone. Twenty past ten. 7% left. Ahv an idea tae head tae Café Tibo, where me an Sonia go before the gemm when she gets me Ivan's ticket. Best place in the town, she always says.

Ahv a windae seat. Hen's teeth they are when there's a gemm on, but it's quiet this mornin, different vibe, no the Green-an-White ahm used tae. Menu looks great. Ahm tryin tae mind how much money ahv goat tae pay day an attemptin no tae salivate too much ower *scallops wi Stornoway black pudding* in case ah realise it's a roll-on-egg day rather than a fuckin-fancy-pants day.

Tae hell, ahl go for it. The night before's still surgin roon ma body, so a decent feed's in order before ah even start tae hink about headin back up the road. It'll gie the phone time tae charge up an aw.

When the food arrives, it looks amazin. Ah ordered an egg too, good for a hangover. Big plunger ae coffee. An two slices ae toast. A treat.

The noise fae ootside burrs through the huge windae behind me. Buses pulse. Slices ae conversation in the street. Inside, almost every table is hushed. Somewhere up the three sterrs at the back there's occasional laughs—but even they're muted. The only outbursts come fae the coffee machine.

Café Tibo. The new Dennistoun. First time Sonia brought me here ah hated it. No the coffee or the grub, but the fact the whole place had changed. Full ae fuckin musicians an students. Nuhin wrang wi them, ahm no sayin that, just different fae the wee while ah stayed here. When it was a greasy pie fae Grant's.

Grant's is still there. Could've gone in ah suppose.

But they scallops were magic.

Ahv a few auld pals in Dennistoun. Fae then. When hings were on the up. Not so much auld *pals* but, just pals at wan time.

The breakfast is gone in a flash. Ah slug the last ae the coffee an refill the mug. Ah close ma eyes, let the warmth move in aroon ma belly. Ma heid's poundin, but ah know the cure is on its way. Ah gulp doon half the mug ae coffee in a oner. Merr warmth, even in ma heid noo.

Ah hink ah might've fell asleep for a minute. It's like ahm no really here.

Ah go up tae the counter an pay the lassie.

'If ah stick a quid on that, will you…'

She says, 'Aye,' before ahv even finished.

An then she says, 'Was that alright for…'

An ah jump in, 'Aye.'

Ah laugh an she laughs. She's got a great wee laugh, kindae bouncy an light.

Friendly, takin the piss oot ae each other.

'Cheers, pal.'

'Cheers to you too,' and she gives me a wee wave as ah head for the door.

When ahm oot ontae Duke street, ah decide to go back tae see Eileen. It's all-day visitin apart fae mealtimes, so ahl be able tae walk up tae the Royal an get in before they shut at hauf-twelve. Twenty minutes'll probably do me anyway. Do Eileen too, the poor auld cunt.

She's no in the bed when ah get tae the ward. Ah pick up the *Daily Record* fae the windae sill an grab a chair. Back pages are full ae Kilmarnock. Ah fold it ontae ma knee an sit there, lookin roon at the different lumps ae bodies in the beds.

When Eileen comes back in, she's bein helped along by a nurse, big athletic fella. She smiles her wide smile.

'Good tae see ye, Allan. Long time too.'

'Aye, ye'll be fed up ae the sight ae me,' ah say.

'Never. Was the gemm good?'

'So-so.' No point in lettin on.

'How'd we dae?'

Ah hold the paper up. 'Humped by Killie.'

'Jesus Christ,' she says.

The nurse guides her gently onto the edge ae the bed.

"You Eileen's nephew?'

'More ae a cousin.'

'Right. Saw you were in yesterday.'

'Aye. No seen her for ages, neither ah huv. Ended up staying the night wi sumbdy, so thought ahl come back in again before headin up the road.'

Eileen shuffles up the bed an pulls the Tuc biscuits oot fae the cupboard. Ah clock the nurse clocking her an ignoring it. Good man.

'Where's up the road then?'

'Fife,' ah say. 'Moved there years ago.'

'Cool. I'm fae Dunfermline originally.'

'Just at Kincardine me, mate. Married a girl there.'

Ah smile at Eileen. 'Ye mind Karen, Eileen?'

'Aye, she was a smashin lassie that, so she wis.'

The nurse picks the Tuc packet up an puts it back intae the cupboard.

'Enough for the day, Eileen, eh pal?'

Eileen laughs. 'Aye, nae bother, nurse.'

GRANDA'S HIP FLASK

Colette Coen

Louise's garden still had a basketball hoop and brown patches on the lawn where there should be grass. She took a gulp of prosecco and tried not to cry. A minute before, her garden had been full of handsome young men: sharp suited, new shoes, ties coordinated with pocket squares. They had been here often in their party gear, though now they drank beer instead of Fruit Shoots. They nudged and bumped each other just the same, only settling for a quick round of photos, to be posted immediately by their mothers.

The taxis pulled up right on time and with a final downing, beer bottles were dropped, and they were gone. The mums had followed them into the street, waving them off and taking more embarrassing photographs, before wandering along to their cars where they stood talking out of Louise's earshot.

Marie hooked her arm through Louise's and led her and Hafsa back into the garden. 'Well ladies,' she said, 'our work here is done.'

'Lucky you,' Hafsa said, 'I've still got another

two to get through school. I swear, these kids will be the death of me.'

'Look at the mess they've made,' Louise said, forcing herself to concentrate on the now and trying not to remember the childish laughter, long ago faded to silence. 'Just dropping everything at their backsides, as usual. Come on girls, help me do a quick tidy and then we'll open another bottle.'

Hafsa swept the cans and bottles off the garden table and into a cooler box before carrying it to the recycling bin. She tipped them in with a clatter while Marie and Louise patrolled the garden, lifting debris from the grass and shrubbery.

'Who was smoking? I didn't think any of them smoked?'

'Oh,' Louise said, 'that butt's maybe mine.'

'When did you start smoking?'

'Well, a wee cheeky one doesn't do you any harm, does it?'

'Yes,' her friends said in unison.

Louise deflected their scorn. 'Maybe we shouldn't have let them drink so much here.'

'It just looks a lot because there were so many of them. Can you believe how much space they take up now? I didn't recognise half the wee boys that used to run about our garden every weekend.'

'The hotel will be strict, won't they? Since it's a school prom,' Hafsa said.

'Do you really believe that? Most of them are over 18 anyway.'

Louise wiped the table and signalled for the others to sit down. 'Jack took my granda's hip flask, so they better not be confiscating things.'

'Oh, you'll never see that again. I gave Mairead my granny's ring to wear to her prom and it managed to vanish. I mean, how do you lose a ring that was on your finger?'

'Was it costly?' Hafsa asked.

'No, just paste, and she had hundreds of them. House full of tat. I wouldn't trust Mairead with anything valuable, even now. I don't know how she remembers to keep people alive at her work.'

'I was going to stop him,' Louise said, her mind going back to the dusty hip flask, 'but I suppose the old man would have approved. It's been lying in a cupboard for years, and at least now it's being used. I just hope he didn't pinch any of Rick's malt to go in it: that, I'd never hear the end of.'

'More likely Crazy Juice,' Marie said, laughing. 'Have you tried that Mad Dog; it's disgusting.'

'I worry about them. I used to just worry about the girls, but now it's Arjan too.'

'I really don't think you'll have any problems, Hafsa, your boy doesn't even drink. He's the sensible one, keeping our boys safe.'

'It's different for him. I can't settle when he's

out. You just don't know what might happen. It only takes one idiot; that's what scares me.'

'Don't worry,' Louise said, briefly touching her friend's hand, 'they'll look after each other. Now girls, cocktails, mocktails? Do you know, I thought more of the other mums would stay?'

'I think one of the girls' mums was having a barbecue,' Hafsa said.

'Did we miss the invite?' Marie said, feigning disgust.

'Not in with the in-crowd,' Louise said. 'God, it reminds me of school. I was too swotty.'

'I was too fat.'

'I was too brown.'

'Sod them,' Louise said, lifting her glass, 'here's to us.'

'To our boys' Hafsa added.

'To the future. Oh Louise, shit, I didn't mean to make you cry.'

'I can't believe Jack's moving away. I've just got the summer with him, and then he'll be gone.'

Marie put a handful of peanuts in her mouth and talked through them. 'Just think, there'll be food in the fridge and none of that charming teenage boy smell. When Aidan left, my shopping bill halved.'

'But Sean is staying home, and you've still got your girls.' Louise began to fold and refold her paper napkin before beginning to tear it into shreds.

Hafsa tried to reassure her. 'A son never really leaves his mother.'

'Maybe not in your culture, but Jack's already talking about a year abroad and American summer camps. I'll be lucky if I see him more than a couple of times a year.'

'They need to grow up. In fact, I wish Sean was moving away; it might give him a bit more sense.'

'Just think of all the time you'll have,' Hafsa said. 'I can't wait until I can stop running about after them. No more parents' nights; no more expensive school trips.'

'No more ironing his shirts,' Marie continued, 'no more gym kits in the hall. And at least you don't have girls stealing your shoes and make-up. And my God, the number of photos they take—but when I take a photo, oh it's got to be approved before I get anywhere near my feed. Thirteen, Aoife is, and you'd think she was trying out to be the next Kardashian.'

Louise looked into her glass. 'I always wanted a girl. Stripy tights and cord pinafores.' She shrugged her shoulders. 'And then you get to take them out for afternoon tea. You don't get that with boys.'

'You don't get the drama either. Tell her, Hafsa, girls are a million times more trouble than boys.'

Hafsa laughed. 'When God wants to punish you, he gives you daughters.'

'That is so cruel,' Louise said. 'I feel guilty now. I do love my boy, but a wee girl would have been lovely.'

'Did you try?' Marie asked.

'Tried to persuade Rick,' Louise said, 'but he was having none of it. He got the snip without even telling me just in case he lost the fight. My God, the look on your faces.'

'That wasn't fair.'

'No,' Louise said, 'but what can you do? Come on, another drink?'

'Am I going to have to cook for your husbands? The two of you are pickled.'

'They prefer your food anyway, Hafsa,' Marie said.

'Why don't we give the boys a call? Wait, not our boy boys, our husband boys. We can phone for a takeaway, and one of them can pick it up. It'll make the night pass quicker; less time to worry about what's happening at the hotel.'

Marie poured another orange juice for Hafsa and emptied what remained of a prosecco bottle into Louise's glass before opening another one. 'Some of the kids have booked rooms, you know.'

'No,' Louise said.

'Why would their parents allow that?' Hafsa couldn't hide her disbelief.

'Oh, there's going to be dozens in each room,' Marie went on.

'As if that will stop them.'

'What have they got to look forward to when they're older?' Louise said. 'I didn't stay in a hotel until I had a job, and even then, it was because my work paid for it. You know, I remember walking Jack to school for his first day. He looked like a wee businessman in his black blazer. I got all upset, and he just walked off without even a wave.'

'I remember,' Marie said. 'I took you for a coffee.'

'You did.'

'Tell Hafsa about the end of the day, though.'

Louise smiled at the memory. 'Well, I'd been sitting half the day telling Marie, who I had never spoken to before that day, all about how useless I felt, such a rubbish mum whose kid wasn't crying at the thought of leaving me. Did I even say that I didn't know how I would fill my time? Stop laughing.'

'Anyway,' Marie said, 'I take this quivering wreck back to the school gates when they finished and Jack comes running out of school and straight into her arms and said *My teacher is the best teacher ever, but you are the best mummy.*'

'Yeah, then you started crying and said, *why have none of my kids ever said that to me?*' Louise took a deep breath. 'But you know something, we've raised good kids and I think things are going to be okay.'

'Yeah,' Marie replied. 'We might not be needed at the school gates anymore, but we'll stick together. And just think, they might all have failed their exams and not be able to leave us after all.'

Louise laughed. 'Now, that would be scary.'

Notes on Authors

Christine Appleyard started writing short stories four years ago when studying Creative Writing with the Open University. She continued writing during her time at Stirling University where she graduated with an M. Litt. in Creative Writing. Her dissertation focussed on linked short stories set in Glasgow. 'Three Stages of Twilight' is the second story of the collection, 'Narrative Art'.

Colette Coen has been published widely, most recently in *Southlight*, *Popshot* and *Postbox*. Her books are available on Amazon. She lives in East Renfrewshire with her husband and their three adult(ish) children. Colette is a proofreader and editor and runs Beech Editorial Services. Follow her at http://colettecoen.wordpress.com

Charlie Gracie grew up in Baillieston, Glasgow. His poetry collections, *Good Morning* (2010), and *Tales from the Dartry Mountains* (2020), were published by Diehard Press. His first novel, *To Live With What You Are* (2019), was published by Postbox Press. His work has appeared in a range of anthologies and journals (including previously in *Postbox* magazine), with some listed for literary prizes, including the Bath Novel Award, Cambridge Short Story Prize, Fish Poetry Prize, and Bridport Short Story and

Poetry Prizes. He was the 2020 official Scriever for the Federation of Writers (Scotland) and is a former Chair of the Scottish Writers' Centre. He now lives on the edge of the Trossachs.

Carol McKay was born and brought up in Drumchapel, in Glasgow. Her short stories and poems have been published widely since she took an MLitt in Creative Writing at the Universities of Strathclyde and Glasgow in 2000. She won the Robert Louis Stevenson Fellowship in 2010 and taught Creative Writing through The Open University between 2004 and 2018. PotHole Press published her novels *Incunabulum* (2020) and *White Spirit* (2022) and her pamphlet of poems *Reading the Landscape* was published by Hedgehog Press in 2022. Carol was appointed Scriever of the Federation of Writers (Scotland) in 2023. Her website is https://www.carolmckay.co.uk

Donal McLaughlin is the author of two collections: *an allergic reaction to national anthems & other stories* (Argyll), and *beheading the virgin mary, and other stories* (Dalkey Archive). He has represented the City of Glasgow in both Berne (Scottish Writing Fellow) and Nuremberg (Hermann Kesten Fellow).